# THE FIRST OLYMPICS

BY BEN M. BAGLIO

*An Edward Packard Book*

ILLUSTRATED BY LESLIE MORRILL

BANTAM BOOKS
TORONTO • NEW YORK • LONDON • SYDNEY • AUCKLAND

THE FIRST OLYMPICS

*A Bantam Book / March 1988*

*CHOOSE YOUR OWN ADVENTURE* " *is a registered trademark of
Bantam Books. Registered in U.S. Patent and Trademark
Office and elsewhere.*

*Original conception of Edward Packard*

ISBN 0-553-27063-X

*Published simultaneously in the United States and Canada*

---

*Bantam Books are published by Bantam Books, a division of Bantam
Doubleday Dell Publishing Group, Inc. Its trademark, consisting of the
words "Bantam Books" and the portrayal of a rooster, is Registered in
U.S. Patent and Trademark Office and in other countries. Marca Regis-
trada. Bantam Books, 666 Fifth Avenue, New York, New York 10103.*

---

PRINTED IN THE UNITED STATES OF AMERICA

O     0 9 8 7 6 5 4 3 2 1

# THE FIRST OLYMPICS

# WARNING!!!

Do not read this book straight through from beginning to end. These pages contain many different adventures you may have during your visit to the first Olympic games. From time to time as you read along, you will be asked to make a choice. Your choice may lead to success or disaster!

The adventures you take are the result of your choice. You are responsible because you choose! After you make your choice, follow the instructions to see what happens to you next.

Think carefully as you compete in the ancient games. You could become an Olympic champion . . . if you make the right choices!

Good luck!

# A Note to the Reader

No one is certain exactly when the first Olympics were held. The games originated as part of a religious festival in western Greece. Over the course of many years, this festival grew in size and importance. Games were added; temples, buildings, and athletic facilities were constructed; and the popularity of the Olympics spread throughout the entire ancient world. The first recorded Olympic games were held in 776 B.C., but the Olympics reached their peak around 500 B.C., which is the approximate setting for this book.

*The First Olympics* remains fairly accurate in reconstructing the ancient games. In ancient Greece, however, no females were permitted anywhere on the sacred Olympic plain—either as athletes or as spectators. This was such a strict rule that any female found at Olympia was pushed off a nearby cliff! Also, the Olympic athletes were required to compete wearing no clothing at all. This tradition is said to have arisen from an instance where a woman, dressed as a man, was found among the contestants. From that point on, all athletes had to forsake clothing during the games.

"And on your right are the remains of the Hippodrome, where the Olympic horse-and-chariot races were held."

It's early morning and you and Felix, your pain-in-the-neck little cousin, are following a guide through the ruins at Olympia, the site of the ancient Olympic games in western Greece. You've looked forward to this summer vacation for a long time, and you've been especially eager to visit Olympia. You'd expected to see glittering temples and impressive stadiums. But as you look around, all you see is a jumble of fallen columns and some wild olive trees. Is this really where the greatest athletes of the ancient world sought glory and honor on the playing field?

The tour guide announces a break for taking pictures, and your group splits up and wanders off in different directions. You decide you want to look around by yourself, and avoid Felix. He broke your camera on the first day of the trip, and ever since then, he's been a real pest.

You walk off in the direction of a low hill. You know from your tour guide that this is the Hill of Cronus. Spectators at the ancient Olympics stood on this hill to watch the athletic competitions. You figure it would be a good place for you to view the entire Olympic plain.

As you climb you notice what looks like the entrance to a cave up ahead. The opening is small, just big enough for you to walk through. You move closer and decide to take a look inside.

*Turn to page 2.*

## 2

You walk into the darkness of the cave. Suddenly, you feel an icy chill that makes you shudder. A sharp wind blows sand into your face, and you cover your eyes from the stinging blast. Then, just as abruptly as they began, the wind and chill are gone.

Maybe coming into the cave wasn't such a good idea. You turn around and walk back outside. But something's wrong! Instead of ancient ruins you see a cluster of columned stone buildings at the base of the hill you just climbed. And at the center of the Olympic plain an ivory-white temple gleams in the sun. It looks a lot like the Parthenon, the massive marble ruin you'd seen in Athens, earlier in your trip. But this temple looks almost new! There are a dozen other buildings of various sizes, and the grounds between them look green and well-cared for.

Amazed, you turn back to look at the cave. The opening in the side of the hill has disappeared!

What's happened? Is it possible that the cave has somehow transported you back to ancient Greece? Before you have a chance to look around some more, two men dressed in togas approach you. You look down and discover that you're dressed the same way.

*Go on to the next page.*

"Hurry!" the bearded man on the left says to you. "The procession to the temple of Zeus is about to begin." He points to a large group of people gathered in the distance. "Surely you don't want to miss it."

You're excited at the chance to stay in ancient Greece, yet frightened. How will you get back to your own time? You see an entrance to a cave in the distance, but it looks quite different from the one you came through. Can you risk staying in ancient Greece for a while before trying to find your way home?

*If you decide to stay for the procession, turn to page 10.*

*If you decide to investigate the cave entrance right away, turn to page 58.*

You wake at dawn the next morning and walk to the Palestra with Athos. Already a crowd of fans has gathered outside the building. You feel the excitement in the air as you approach the special arch reserved for athletes.

But just as you're about to enter the building, you spot a hunchbacked old woman in a faded toga who has been pushed to the ground by the crowd. Her face is half hidden by shadow, but the part you can see is almost too ugly to look at. You help her to her feet.

"Thank you. Unlike all the others, you are kind. I want to reward you with a gift," the old woman says with a cackle. "Charms to help you at Olympia." She reaches into an old canvas pouch and pulls out a small brass medal in the shape of a lion. "Put this around your neck, and it will bring you strength," the woman says, holding the medal by its leather thong. Again she reaches into the pouch. This time she pulls out a medal with a rainbow carved onto it. "But this medal will bring you incredible luck," she says. "You can have only one. Which will you choose?"

*If you choose the lion-shaped medal, turn to page 30.*

*If you choose the medal with the rainbow, turn to page 43.*

A minute later the wind dies suddenly, and it becomes terribly still within the chamber. The light above the priestess returns to gold, and you see that she has come out of her trance. She lowers her head to look at you, her eyes shining with understanding. In a solemn voice just above a whisper she says:

"I've had a vision of the *pankration* pit,
I'll tell what I've seen, and this is it:
Victory is woven upon Fate's loom,
But surrounding the victory there is doom."

Before you can ask the priestess to explain, the light in the recess dims, and she disappears in the darkness. Once again the wind rushes into the chamber with a sound like voices. But now the voices are saying something perfectly clear: "Go!"

As quickly as you can, you rush up the stairs and toward the entrance of the cavern. You're about to run into the pine grove when, suddenly, the moonlight shines on an object at your feet. It's your lion medal, and it doesn't appear to have been damaged at all by the magic flames!

*Go on to the next page.*

You wonder whether you should take the medal with you. After all, the strength it gives you would certainly help in the *pankration*. But to consult the oracle, you were supposed to sacrifice your most valuable possession. Who knows what might happen if you took it back? Still, the medal is just lying there, and there's no one around. Who would know if you reached down and took it?

*If you decide to take the medal,
turn to page 38.*

*If you leave the medal where you found it,
turn to page 94.*

"What about letting me race your chariot?" you suggest. "I may not be the best charioteer in the world, but I'm a fast learner. If you could teach me the basics, maybe with a little luck we'll win that race."

Leon looks at you, smiling for the first time. "You know," he says, his voice filled with hope, "that just might work. My horses are very obedient and as swift as the wind. It shouldn't be too difficult to turn you into a driver. Anyway, it's our only hope of saving Marissa."

Leon leads you past the Hippodrome to the stables. He opens the door to one of them and you go inside. There, in adjoining stalls, are four of the biggest and most beautiful stallions you've ever seen. They're pure white, with proud faces and strong, muscular bodies. The horses whinny softly as Leon approaches.

"They run like panthers, but are as gentle as kittens," Leon says, feeding a handful of straw to one of the stallions. The horse nestles against him and nudges him with his nose.

"Come," Leon says to you, "let's take the horses outside and teach you something about chariot racing."

*Turn to page 18.*

You step behind some bushes and wait until the man with the scar passes you. He walks briskly back in the direction of the Temple of Zeus, then turns right. You're glad to see that a number of people have come down from the hill onto the Olympian plain. Now you can follow the scarred man closely without him suspecting.

He leads you to a long, columned building, which you saw on your tour. It's the Leonidaeum, where the wealthy Olympic visitors stay. It makes sense that Demonicus would hold Marissa there, you think. After all, he wouldn't want to keep her out in the open where she might escape. And if he was able to hire Nikos of Sparta away from Leon, he certainly must be rich enough to afford a room or two in the Leonidaeum.

A guard stands at the gates to the building. He nods as the man with the scar approaches, then he opens the gates and lets the man pass through.

How are you going to get past the guard? you wonder. Perhaps you could pretend to be a messenger and try to trick the guard into letting you into the Leonidaeum. But what if he doesn't believe you? Maybe you'd be better off searching for another way into the building.

*If you attempt to trick the guard by pretending to be a messenger, turn to page 52.*

*If you decide to look for another way in, turn to page 42.*

You nod to the men in togas and begin making your way down the hill to where the athletes have gathered for the procession. As you walk, you notice that everyone seems to be having a lot of fun. A pair of jugglers toss apples high into the air as the watching crowd gasps in amazement. A smaller group surrounds a singer, who strums a stringed lyre and sings a song about Hercules. The music sounds tuneless to you, but you applaud with the others when the song is over, just to be polite. The ancient Olympics aren't nearly as solemn as you had thought.

A peddler tries to sell you a wreath made from an olive branch, telling you, "It's just like the ones to be won by the Olympic champions." You find it hard to believe that souvenirs were sold more than two thousand years ago!

"The tour of Olympia is about to begin," a gray-haired man calls out. "Come and see all the sights, and learn about the athletes that have made the Olympics famous," he cries. "Mine is the only complete tour of Olympia!"

It might be helpful to find out more about the Olympics and to learn your way around. But maybe you should continue on to where the athletes have gathered for the procession to the Temple of Zeus.

*If you decide to take the tour of Olympia, turn to page 55.*

*If you keep heading toward the procession, turn to page 68.*

## 12

In the torchlight you see that Leon had managed to take apart a portion of the chariot but didn't have time to put it back together. It takes only one look at the disassembled chariot for the men to guess that you were trying to sabotage it.

The two men tie your hands behind your back and lead you to the temple of Zeus. You're brought before the *Hellanodicae,* the seven stern-looking high priests of Olympia, and accused of trying to fix the chariot race.

You don't have much to offer in your defense. You don't want to mention Leon because it would spoil his chances of winning his daughter back in the race. And you can't deny trying to tamper with the chariot. After all, you've been caught red-handed. Your only hope is that the *Hellanodicae* aren't too hard on you.

*Turn to page 107.*

By steeling yourself, you manage to hold your own in the competition. Half an hour later you and Athos are still in the *skamma* with the match tied at two falls each. Your muscles are burning with pain, and you're tempted to give up. But if you hold out just a little longer, you might win the tournament.

The crowd is wild, cheering and shouting. Just as they think Athos is going to drive you to the ground, you manage to escape his hold. And just when they're certain that Athos's strength is about to run out, he comes back with more energy than ever. Finally, Athos locks his arms around your head and attempts to buckle your knees with his foot. You know the end is near, but you can't allow Athos to defeat you. You grab his arm, and with your last bit of strength, force him to release his hold. You've escaped! Just then the purple-robed official enters the *skamma* and stops the match.

The official addresses the crowd in a loud voice: "Good people of Greece," he says, "today we set out to find which of these two youths is the best wrestler in the world. After having watched this magnificent display of strength and courage, I hope you will agree with me that both wrestlers deserve to be crowned as victors."

The crowd roars in approval. "Then," the official cries, "let the victory celebration begin!"

*Turn to page 56.*

"How did *you* get here?" you whisper quickly to Felix.

"There was this . . . this cave," he stammers. "I walked into it and everything changed."

Leave it to Felix to follow you to ancient Greece! you think. It's just your luck to be stuck with him.

But when the official lowers his hand and signals for you to start wrestling, you realize that the charm has brought you good luck after all. For the moment, it doesn't matter whether you go on to win the entire wrestling tournament or not. Using the "hoisting high" move to throw Felix to the ground will be victory enough for you! You just hope that after you beat him, Felix will lead you back to the cave.

**The End**

# 16

You might be able to defeat Athos without wearing the lion-shaped medal, but you're not about to take any chances. This is your one big opportunity to win at Olympia.

An official in a purple robe calls you and Athos into the *skamma*. With one hand he clasps your shoulder. He places his other hand on Athos's shoulder. "May the best wrestler win," he announces in a loud voice.

The official walks away from the *skamma* and gives the signal for you to begin wrestling. The crowd begins to shout and cheer. Some people are calling your name, others are cheering for Athos, but most just seem to be yelling in excitement.

You decide to take advantage of Athos's worn-out state by making the first move. Crouching, you lunge toward him, slip your left hand behind his left knee, and jerk your arm upward. Athos is taken completely by surprise and falls to the sand with a groan.

Athos gets to his feet, looking completely exhausted. Yet you feel stronger than ever. You think that after you've won the olive crown you should look for the old woman who gave you the lion medal and try to repay her in some way.

*Go on to the next page.*

Next you decide to trick Athos into thinking that you're just as tired as he is. You allow him to get a solid grip around your waist from behind, and you offer little resistance as he places his right hand behind your neck. Just as Athos is about to drive you to the sand, you lean forward, place your left hand behind you, and flip him forward, over your shoulders and onto the ground.

As you flip Athos, you don't notice that he has grabbed hold of the leather thong around your neck that holds your medal in place. As he falls, the thin leather strip breaks with a snap, and you see the medal fly into the sand!

*Turn to page 59.*

# 18

After you and Leon have bridled the horses, you pull the chariot out from its storage compartment in the stable. The chariot is nothing more than a low three-sided cart mounted on a set of small wheels. It looks awfully flimsy to you.

"Are you sure this chariot can win?" you ask.

"Don't worry," Leon assures you. "I built it myself."

You hitch the stallions to the chariot and climb inside. Leon leads you out to the Hippodrome, where other chariot drivers have begun to practice.

"That is the starting gate," Leon says, pointing to a V-shaped structure at one end of the course. In front of the gate is an altar with a bronze eagle on it. "Tomorrow, each of the chariots will take its place in one of the gate's compartments with a rope stretched across its front. When the race is about to start, a trumpet will sound and the eagle will fly upward. Then the ropes in the starting gate will be released and the race will begin.

"In order to finish the race," Leon explains, "you must drive the chariot up and down the course and around the center poles at each end twenty-four times."

*Turn to page 24.*

As soon as the two men have left the stable you tiptoe to the door, unlatch it as quietly as you can, and slip outside. You hide behind a pillar until the men get about twenty yards away. Then, trying your hardest not to make a sound, you start to follow them.

You trail the men past the Hippodrome and in the direction of the Hill of Cronus. You're relieved to see that most of the time they're talking to each other and not paying much attention to anything else.

The sun is rising. In the distance a number of people have awoken at their campsites on the hill. Most of the spectators at the Olympic festivals have to sleep outdoors. Only the athletes and very wealthy visitors are allowed to spend the night inside on the Olympic grounds.

At last, the two men reach the base of the Hill of Cronus, and you're certain it won't be long before you know where Demonicus is hiding Leon's daughter. Then something happens which makes your stomach sink: the men wave good-bye to each other and head off in opposite directions. The man with the long black hair and shaggy beard starts to walk up the hill, while the man with the curly hair and the scarred cheek turns back toward the Olympian plain. Which one will lead you to Marissa?

*If you try to follow the bearded man, turn to page 65.*

*If you try to follow the man with the scar, turn to page 9.*

You open the stable door and duck inside. It's pitch-dark, and there's no sign of Leon. You're sure that he has escaped with his lantern. But where is the exit?

The footsteps outside are getting closer, and now you hear men's voices. As your eyes grow used to the darkness, you start to look for a place to hide. You think you see a haystack at the end of the stable. Quietly you tiptoe toward it.

Everything goes wrong all at once. Your foot bangs into something hard and you trip, falling against Demonicus's chariot with a tremendous crash. Two men carrying torches rush into the stable before you have a chance to get up and hide. The light from the torches shines into your eyes and illuminates your face and the surrounding area.

*Turn to page 12.*

You crack your whip, and your team of white stallions bolts from the starting gate. The crowd lets loose a deafening cheer. With one hand you hold on tightly to the frame of the chariot, with the other, you clasp the reins.

Swift as lightning, your horses immediately put you ahead of the eleven other chariots. After half a length of the course, only one chariot seems to be close to yours—Demonicus's!

You crack your whip again, and the horses respond instantly, running even faster. The wind whips back your hair, and a sense of exhilaration rises up in you as you approach the pole at the end of the field. You pull on the reins a little to avoid tipping over the chariot as you make a tight turn. Then you start to head back up the racecourse.

You quickly glance behind and see Nikos of Sparta furiously whipping Demonicus's horses. Then you turn your full attention to the field ahead of you. The other chariots are now coming straight at you, and you have to be careful to avoid a collision.

You guide the chariot to the extreme right of the course, away from the approaching pack. But in drawing so far to the right, you've lost momentum. Through a cloud of dust you see that Nikos is taking a more dangerous route closer to the center of the field. And he's closing the gap between you— shortening your lead!

*Turn to page 110.*

You dash down the length of the stables, away from the footsteps. You're pretty sure that no one has seen you, but you continue to run until you reach Leon's stable. You're sweating and out of breath.

Leon is waiting for you there, and he's happy to see you. "That was close," he says. "But I wasn't able to sabotage the chariot before you signaled for me to get away. There's no way I'll be able to win against Nikos now." With his head down he walks over to his team of white stallions and feeds a handful of straw to one of the horses.

He looks so miserable you decide to take the risk you weren't willing to take earlier.

"Let me race your chariot, Leon," you say. "I've never driven before, but we have all day tomorrow for me to learn how. Maybe with some luck, I can win your daughter back."

Leon's face lights up with a huge grin. Standing straight and proud, he strides over to you and claps an arm on your shoulder. "You're on!" he exclaims. "We're going to make the finest charioteer out of you that Olympia has ever seen!"

*Turn to page 82.*

You spend all that day learning how to control the horses and steer the chariot. The small chariot seems as reliable as Leon claimed, and the white stallions are swift and obedient. With a little more practice you just might be a match for Nikos of Sparta.

Late in the afternoon, you and Leon lead the horses to the stable. A small group of men is blocking the entrance. All of them look mean, but one looks far meaner and more sinister than the rest. He has a bald head and dark, glaring eyes. "Demonicus," Leon whispers to you.

*Turn to page 60.*

"Okay, Felix," you say. "Let's go!"

Marissa wishes you luck, and the two of you start to run toward the Hippodrome, following the path you'd driven along the day before. After a few minutes of sprinting, the racecourse comes into view. But before you arrive at the entrance, the last chariot enters the Hippodrome, and the gates slam shut behind it.

"Now look what's happened!" you shout at Felix, certain that somehow it's his fault. "I never should have brought you along." Your mind is racing, and you desperately look for a way inside.

"Hey, I've got an idea!" Felix shouts. And before you can say another word, your little cousin has squeezed through the bars of the gate.

"Felix, that's great! Now open the gate for me!" The chariots are nearing the starting line. There's no time to spare.

Felix struggles with the heavy metal latch. "Hurry!" you cry. "We're running out of time!"

The seconds it takes Felix to raise the latch seem like hours. Finally he pulls open the gate wide enough for you to slip through. "Now wait here!" you cry as you race for the V-shaped starting gate.

*Turn to page 51.*

You win match after match in the tournament, and the wrestlers you defeat are eliminated from the contest.

"Perhaps the youth is a god in disguise," a woman says to the man next to her after you've beaten a very strong opponent.

The competition continues into the late afternoon, and you beat every competitor you face. The medal's powers seem as strong as ever, and you're learning more and more about wrestling strategy.

Your victories have qualified you for the final round. You're pleased to find that your friend Athos has also had a successful day and has made it through the tournament to the finals.

Now it's your turn to wrestle against Athos. The winner of this round will be declared the Olympic champion. In the break before the match begins, you take a look at Athos. He's exhausted. Sweat runs down his face, and his shoulders are slumped. It's clear that he doesn't have much strength left after wrestling all day. Athos taught you many of the moves that you used to win today. Is it fair to wear the lion-shaped medal when you wrestle him? you wonder. Maybe you should take it off. But when you wrestled against Athos yesterday, you managed to score only a draw. Can you defeat him without the medal?

---

*If you decide to continue wearing the medal, turn to page 16.*

*If you decide that it wouldn't be fair to rely on the medal's powers, turn to page 92.*

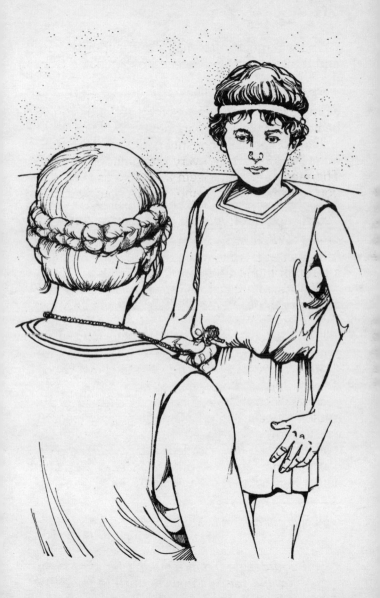

# 28

You and Athos move to one of the large open-
air rooms of the Palestra. There you meet a trainer
who goes over the rules of wrestling with you. You
learn that most wrestling in the ancient Olympics is
done in a standing position. To win a match, you
must throw your opponent to the ground three
times. Tripping and holds on all parts of the body
are not penalized. Big wrestlers have an advantage, you realize, because there don't seem to be
any weight classes in the wrestling competitions.

After the rules have been explained, you feel
sure enough of yourself to challenge Athos to a
practice match.

*Turn to page 34*.

You reach up and touch something that feels like a leafy hat. Taking it off, you see that it's a crown woven from branches of some sort.

"Where did you find it?" Felix asks. "Can I get one, too?"

You try as hard as you can to recall how the crown got on your head. But the last thing you remember was leaving your tour group and walking up the Hill of Cronus. "I don't know," you say, running your finger across the gray-green leaves. "I don't know."

**The End**

You put the lion-shaped medal around your neck and thank the old woman. Then you enter the Palestra. As you walk, you feel a strange surge of confidence. You're not sure whether it's the medal or the excitement of being in the Olympics that's making you feel this way.

You take your place among the athletes. The large crowd gathered in the courtyard of the Palestra cheers as an official welcomes all the athletes to Olympia. He calls out names and divides the wrestlers into two groups. Then he instructs one group to draw the names of their opponents from a silver urn he is holding.

Athos wrestles first and easily wins his match over a youth from the island of Crete. Then it's your turn. You put oil and sand on your body and enter the *skamma*. Your opponent, Hector, from Sparta, is taller than you and has powerful muscles that ripple in the bright sunlight. You can only hope that your wrestling skills and the lion medal you are wearing will bring you victory.

The official signals for you to start wrestling. Hector lunges for your waist and tries to pick you up and throw you to the ground. But when he tightens his arms around you, you press all of your weight downward. As Hector struggles to lift you, you grab him under the arms and push him backward as hard as you can. He releases his grip on your waist and crashes to the ground.

The crowd gasps in amazement. Even you are surprised. Is it possible that the old woman's medal could bring you such strength?

*Turn to page 49.*

You tell the official that you want to ask the Olympic oracle about the *pankration*. "But how do I do that?" you ask.

"Tonight you must wait until the goddess Diana has driven her moon chariot into the sky," the official whispers, drawing you close. "Then you must walk along the path that leads to the gates of Olympia. When you reach a grove of pine trees, locate the stars which make up Orion the hunter, and walk in the direction of Orion's shield. Soon you will reach the cavern of the oracle. You will know it from the magical fire which blocks the entrance.

"Before you can enter the sacred cavern and speak to the priestess within, you must first make a sacrifice of your most treasured possession," the official continues. "Throw it into the center of the flames, and if it is acceptable, the fire will die down and you can safely enter the cavern."

*Turn to page 40.*

Just as you're about to reach for the handle, the door opens abruptly. A buxom woman is standing there—she looks like a heavyweight wrestler. Before you have a chance to run, she grabs your arm. "Help!" she yells. "Guards! There's a burglar in my room, trying to steal my jewels!"

In an instant, two guards seize you by the shoulders. You try squirming out of their grasp, but it's no use. You insist you haven't done anything wrong, but they don't listen to you. They tie your hands behind your back and drag you off to be tried as a thief.

You have no way to prove your innocence. Unless you can find a way to escape from prison, it'll be years before you get a chance to return to your own time!

## The End

**34**

Before you enter the *skamma* in the center of the room, Athos takes a jar of olive oil from a shelf on the wall. He rubs his body with the oil and then scatters a handful of sand from the pit over his skin. "I find that this gives me a better grip," he explains. You pour out some oil and do the same.

You stand opposite Athos to begin your match. When the trainer drops his hand, you start to circle each other. You're about to grab Athos's leg when suddenly he falls on one knee, grabs your right arm, turns his back to you, and throws you over his shoulder! You land in the sand—hard!—and the trainer awards a point to Athos.

"We call that move 'hoisting high,'" Athos says as you brush the sand off your arms and get to your feet. "Come, I'll teach it to you."

You spend the next few hours learning the "hoisting high" and other moves that the trainer teaches you and Athos. By the end of the day you've improved to the point where a practice match against Athos ends in a draw. You scrape the sand and oil off your body with a curved knife that Athos calls a *strigil* and head for the athletes' quarters. It's time to rest for your match tomorrow.

*Turn to page 5.*

With a blast of trumpets the gates to the Hippodrome swing open, and two purple-robed judges on horseback lead the procession onto the field. The crowd roars with excitement. Your heart pounds in your chest. You give a tug on the reins, and your team of white stallions responds at once, expertly following the chariot in front of you.

When you reach the starting gate, Leon directs you to your assigned stall. Next to you Demonicus is talking to his charioteer, Nikos of Sparta. Demonicus casts an icy glance at you. There's a hint of a smile on his face, but it seems hard and cruel.

"Don't worry about him," Leon says to you. "Concentrate on the race, and you'll do just fine." He steps down from the chariot. "May the gods be with you," he says.

Now all the chariots are in position. Another fanfare of trumpets rings out. With one hand clasping the horses' reins, the other gripped firmly around the whip, you concentrate on the bronze eagle at the front of the starting gate. Suddenly the eagle shoots upward, and the rope at the front of the stall disappears. The race has begun!

*Turn to page 53.*

# 36

At the near end of the racecourse a crowd of people is standing in front of an open-air building. This must be the place to register for the chariot racing, you think. But when you ask where to find a chariot to drive in a race, the man at the registration desk starts to laugh.

"The chariot owners at Olympia selected their drivers months ago," he says. "You can't enter a race now."

Disappointed, you turn away from the desk. But just as you're about to leave, a man with a gray beard and a gold-striped toga calls you over to him.

"I am in great need," the man declares after you sit down next to him. "You must help me."

You ask the man how you can help him, and he continues: "My name is Leon, and I come from Elis, not far from here. The chariot I own was victorious at the last Olympics. A very wealthy and powerful man named Demonicus owned the chariot that finished second. After the race, some of his henchmen seized my beautiful daughter, Marissa, and carried her off. Demonicus swore that the only way I could get her back was to beat him again in the chariot race at the next festival. Otherwise he will marry her and take her far away.

*Go on to the next page.*

"For four years I have waited to see Marissa again. I bought the finest horses and hired Nikos of Sparta, the most famous charioteer in the world. I spared no expense to make certain I would win the race the day after tomorrow. But Demonicus is very crafty. This morning I found out that Demonicus offered my charioteer four times the amount of money I was to pay him. Now he will race for Demonicus!"

*Turn to page 95.*

You reach down to pick up your medal. But as soon as you touch it, a flash of light appears, making the night as bright as day. In a clearing just ahead you see a swirling column of smoke. The smoke begins to take form, and an instant later a tall, noble-looking man with a spectacular dazzling crown on his head appears.

"I am Apollo," he declares in a voice like thunder, "the sun god and the god of prophecy. This is my oracle," he says angrily, "and *that*"—he points to the medal at your feet—"is the sacrifice you made in order to speak to my priestess. How dare you try to take back what you have given to the gods! You are not worthy to wear the Olympic crown," he cries, and instantly the olive wreath on your head crumbles to dust and falls around you. "Be gone from this place!" he commands, raising his arms.

A blast of wind rushes from the cavern and knocks you to the ground. You try to stand up, but the wind is too strong. You look at Apollo and see him disappearing once again in a column of smoke.

*Turn to page 102.*

# 40

That night when the moon has risen, you set out to find the oracle. Clasped firmly in your hand is your most precious possession—the lion-shaped medal that helped you win the wrestling tournament. You follow the official's directions and soon you are in front of the cavern of the oracle.

As the official told you, a wall of fire blocks the entrance. But this is unlike any fire you've ever seen. The flames burn yellow and green and spring from solid rock, yet they don't seem to give off any heat. The fire casts spooky, colored shadows all around you, and the wind whips your hair and makes an unearthly howling sound as it rushes into the cavern. Summoning all of your courage, you walk closer to the fire. You pause for a moment. Then, with a flick of your wrist, you cast the medal into the flames.

*Turn to page 93*.

A few minutes later, Leon arrives at the stable. When he asks how everything went during the night, you tell him that there was no sign of Demonicus or his men. You don't mention that you weren't awake for most of the time you were supposed to be keeping watch.

You lead the horses outside, bridle them, and hitch them to the chariot. Just as you finish, you hear the sound of trumpets in the distance. It's time for all the chariots to gather outside the Hippodrome. The race is about to begin!

You get in the chariot with Leon and set out for the racecourse. Soon you arrive at the gates of the Hippodrome. Eleven other chariots are waiting, and an official tells you where to stop. Before the race begins, each chariot owner and driver will take part in a procession to the starting gate.

From where you stand in the chariot, you can see thousands of spectators gathered on the embankment. It's clear from their wild cries that they're as anxious as you are for the race to begin.

*Turn to page 35.*

# 42

You study the Leonidaeum, trying to figure out how you can get inside without going through the gate.

After a few minutes, you come up with a plan: If you can locate an empty room, you can climb through the window. The windows, which are just rectangular openings in the stone wall, are only about a foot above your head. Once you're inside, it shouldn't be too difficult to find where Demonicus is hiding Marissa.

You walk to the far side of the building, away from the guard at the front entrance. Looking around to make sure no one sees you, you silently approach one of the windows. You listen for sounds inside the room, but you don't hear a thing. You figure that most of the guests at the Leonidaeum are probably out watching the Olympic contests.

You reach above your head, grab hold of the window ledge, and pull yourself up. You don't see anyone in the room, so you swing your legs inside and hop down onto the floor. Then you quickly cross to the door.

*Turn to page 33*.

You put the rainbow-carved charm around your neck and thank the old woman for the gift. Then you rush into the Palestra just in time for the start of the wrestling tournament. Hundreds of people have gathered in the courtyard to watch. You hope that the charm you're wearing will bring you the luck you need to win.

An official in a purple robe welcomes all of the athletes to Olympia. He instructs half of the wrestlers to draw the names of their opponents from a large silver urn he is holding. Athos chooses someone named Theopompus. The name on the slip of paper you've picked is Felicitus. That name sounds familiar. Isn't he the latecomer the fat woman asked you about when you registered yesterday? you think.

Athos wrestles first and wins easily over Theopompus, 3–0. Your turn is next. You rub your body with oil and sand and walk out to the *skamma* to await your opponent.

When Felicitus walks into the sand pit, you gasp in amazement. This isn't a Greek wrestler; it's your cousin Felix, and he looks as surprised as you!

*Turn to page 14.*

"For chariot racing, you must head to the Hippodrome," says Athos. He points in the direction of the racecourse, and you wish each other good luck as you part.

As you walk, you pass hundreds of people who have come to the festival from all parts of Greece. Everyone seems to be talking about a different competition. Listening to their conversations, you can't help feeling excited about the chance to compete in the Olympics.

Just as the Hippodrome comes in sight, a huge parade of bulls forces you off the path. They're chained together in long double columns and are led by four very solemn-looking men in purple robes. "Where are they going?" you ask a woman standing nearby.

"The bulls are to be sacrificed," the woman replies. She explains that at the start of each festival the *Hellanodicae,* high priests of Olympia, lead a hundred bulls to the Temple of Zeus. A sacred rite is held in front of the altar, and the bulls are killed to honor Zeus, the king of the gods. "Later, the meat will be eaten at the victory celebrations," she adds.

You remind yourself to make sure not to pass the Temple of Zeus for the next few hours. You're sure it wouldn't do your appetite much good to see a hundred bulls being slaughtered.

When the last bull has passed, you walk a bit farther and arrive at the Hippodrome, a rectangular dirt field flanked by a grassy embankment. Your heart starts to pound as you realize that this is where you'll be racing a chariot in just a few days!

*Turn to page 36*.

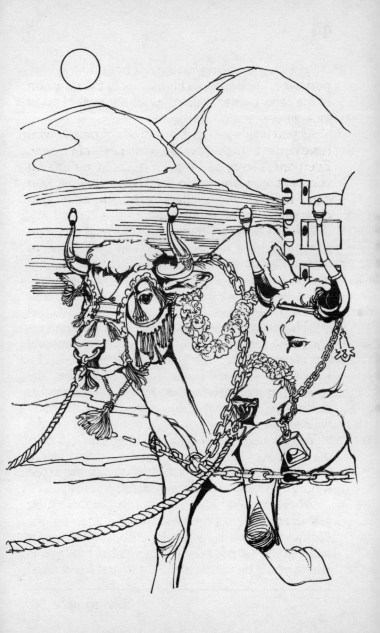

# 46

"Felix, you stay here with Marissa," you say. The last thing you want is your pesky cousin tagging along again. You're sure he'll just make a mess of things. "I'll go alone and meet you back here after I've warned Leon."

Another fanfare of trumpets comes from the direction of the Hippodrome. "That's the signal for the procession into the racecourse to begin," Marissa says anxiously. "You'd better hurry!"

As you turn to leave, you see that Felix looks disappointed about having to stay at the stable. But you're sure you've made the right decision.

You take off, running as fast as you can. You've got to get to the Hippodrome before the race begins, and there's not much time. Once the procession of contestants makes it way through the racecourse, it will only be a matter of minutes before the chariots enter the starting gate. And then it will be too late to save Leon!

The Hippodrome is now in sight, and you run toward the entrance for the chariots. You're about a hundred yards away when you see the last chariot pass through the gates. You're certain there's enough time to stop the race. But just then the gates swing closed!

*Turn to page 54*.

You can always look for the cave later, but you'll never again have the chance to be declared the greatest athlete in the world. You'll compete in the *pankration!*

Early the next morning you tell the gray-bearded official your answer. "A brave decision," he declares. "The oracle must have given you a very encouraging prediction."

You nod, not mentioning anything about the doom the priestess foretold. You've decided not to worry about the oracle's prophecy. No one can predict the future, especially not some creepy woman in a cave.

"The *pankration* events take place at noon to-day," the official says. Then he briefly explains the rules of the competition to you. Like the wrestling events, the *pankration* takes place in the *skamma* of the Palestra. All moves are allowed and all parts of the body may be used in order to try to defeat your opponent. As in Olympic boxing, a competitor is eliminated from the contest either by raising his hand in defeat or by being knocked unconscious. Each match continues until one of the opponents is victorious, and the winners go on to further competitions. Because the *pankration* is so dangerous, it is one of the most popular events among the Olympic spectators.

You agree to be at the Palestra at noon. You're going to try your hardest to win the *pankration.* Soon you'll be declared the best athlete at Olympia!

*Turn to page 112.*

Instead of rushing after the men, everyone around you gasps in horror. But they're not looking at the men in purple togas. They're looking at you!

Your tour guide shakes his head as the two men start to approach you. "First you didn't know who Milo of Croton was," he says to you, "now this. How could anyone not recognize two of the *Hellanodicae,* the high priests at Olympia? That is what their purple robes signify. And those were not swords you saw, but the rods they carry as symbols of their position. You have made a most terrible mistake, and you will certainly be punished. Let us hope the *Hellanodicae* show you mercy."

The two judges are swift in their punishment. They order that you be removed from the Olympic grounds and that you not be allowed to reenter until after the festival is over. You won't get to see any of the events. And you'll have to wait five long and lonely days before you can even try to find the cave through which you were brought back in time—and through which you just might get back to the twentieth century. Meanwhile, you'll have nothing to eat but olives!

**The End**

The official has awarded you for Hector's fall.

With a groan Hector gets to his feet. His face is flushed, and there's an angry look in his eyes. It's clear that he isn't used to being thrown—and that he's not about to allow it to happen again.

Once more Hector stands across the *skamma* from you. He charges across the sand pit like a bull, crouched low to tackle you. But the instant before he reaches you, you step aside, grab hold of his waist, and flip his legs over his head. Hector lands flat on his back.

The crowd cheers and chants your name, and you are awarded another point. You need to score only once more to win the match.

When Hector gets to his feet, his face is even redder and his eyes even angrier than before. As he comes at you, you feel your body tense. Can you put your faith in the medal? You hope its powers don't fail you now.

Hector grasps your arms and pushes downward as hard as he can, trying to force you to the ground. Your feet begin to slip in the sand, but before you collapse, you lock your knees. Then with a burst of strength, you are able to push upward, lifting Hector off the ground and sending him flying through the air. He lands outside the sand pit. You've won the match!

Cheers erupt from the crowd, and you clasp the lion-shaped medal around your neck. With the strength it brings you, you know you can't be defeated. It's only a matter of time before you'll be crowned an Olympic champion!

*Turn to page 26.*

You run alongside the course, determined to reach Leon before the race begins. Already you can see the trumpeter in position next to the starting gate.

Your muscles strain as you try to run even faster. You shout Leon's name as loud as you can, but the cheers of the crowd drown your cries.

The chariots are all in place when you get to one end of the starting gate. You turn and run to Leon's stall. Just as you arrive behind his chariot, the trumpet blares. The race is on!

There's no time for you to think. As the horses bolt from the stall, you jump aboard the chariot and grab the reins from Leon's hands. Leon looks at you in disbelief. "The chariot's been sabotaged!" you yell.

You veer off the course, and rein in the horses. Just then, one wheel of the chariot falls off. You and Leon tumble to the ground, but neither of you is hurt.

"Demonicus's men put wax pins in the chariot's wheels. I didn't have a chance to fix them because I went to look for Marissa," you explain to Leon.

"Marissa!" Leon cries. "Where is she? Is she all right?"

*Turn to page 66.*

You don't know much about how messengers are supposed to act, but you think the best thing would be to look as if you're in a terrific hurry to deliver the message. So once you've thought of something to say, you race toward the guard.

"I've a message for Demonicus, sir," you say in your most serious-sounding voice. "I've run all night long, and I must deliver it at once!"

The guard looks you over, as if trying to decide whether to trust you. "Demonicus, you say? Well, he's already left for the Hippodrome. The chariot race is to begin soon."

Is Marissa with Demonicus or is she inside the Leonidaeum? you wonder. Somehow you've got to find out.

"There are too many people at the Hippodrome," you say. "It might take me hours to find Demonicus. Is there anyone in his room I can leave my message with?"

The guard thinks for a moment. "I'm pretty sure that one of Demonicus's friends just went inside," he says. "And then there's that girl he arrived with a couple of days ago. You know, I haven't seen her leave this building since the start of the festival."

You're certain the guard is talking about Marissa! Now you've simply got to get inside.

"Ah, yes, his handmaiden. She can be trusted," you say slyly. "Can you tell me where his room is? I can't waste any time in delivering this message."

"Very well," the guard replies, and he gives you instructions. Then he opens the gates, and you rush into the Leonidaeum.

*Turn to page 86.*

You crack the whip, and your team of white stallions flies out of the starting gate like a bullet from a gun. Most of the other chariots get off to a much slower start. Only Demonicus's chariot, pulled by four jet-black horses, seems to be a match for you.

You can't hear a sound other than the roar of the crowd and the thunder of the horses' hooves against the ground. But while the noise is deafening, it's also exhilarating, and you urge the horses to gallop even faster.

You maneuver the chariot around the brass pole at the end of the Hippodrome, being careful not to take the turn too quickly. As you guide the horses back down the straight section of the racecourse, you see Nikos of Sparta directly behind you. He is whipping his horses mercilessly, forcing them to catch your chariot. You crack your whip once more, and the white stallions charge ahead.

Just then your chariot starts to rock from side to side. You can barely hold on tight enough to keep from falling out. You tug on the reins, hoping that slowing down some will help, but the rocking continues. Then with a sickening lurch, you feel the chariot drop from below your feet. You see one of your wheels roll down the field as you fall to the ground. Your horses continue to run like the wind, ripping the reins from your hands.

*Turn to page 103.*

"Open up!" you shout through the bars of the gate. There's a guard not far away, and you hope you can catch his attention. But the crowd roars with excitement as the procession of chariots approaches the starting gate. "Open up!" you shout once again, but the guard can't hear you.

You try squeezing through the bars, but you're too big. You can't help thinking that Felix would have been able to get through—*if* you had let him come along.

Just then you hear the sound you'd been dreading—the shrill blast of a lone trumpet. In the next instant you feel the rumble of horses' hooves pounding against the ground. The race has begun!

Then everything seems to happen in slow motion. You run toward the embankment and try to push your way through the screaming spectators. You're determined to get to the officials' stand and enlist their help to stop the race. But there are too many people on the hillside. It seems to take forever for you to move forward just a few yards.

You press on, weaving a path through the crowd. Finally the spot where the purple-robed officials have gathered comes into view. And soon you're just twenty feet away. You scramble desperately over the last few yards.

As you approach the officials' stand, the crowd gasps in unison. For the first time since the race began, you look down at the field. Through a cloud of dust you see a wrecked chariot. Lying in the dirt beside it is Leon, motionless. You're too late.

**The End**

You join the small group gathered in front of the gray-haired tour guide. As the tour begins, he explains that every four years the best athletes from all of the city-states in Greece gather to compete in honor of Zeus, the king of the gods. The Olympic festival will last five days, with the first day—today—devoted to oath taking and sacrifices, the next three days to the athletic contests, and the last day for the final victory procession.

"Throughout all of Greece a truce has been declared especially for the Olympics," the guide tells your group. "All disagreements must be forgotten until everyone returns home safely from the Olympics. It is forbidden to bring weapons to the Olympian plain, and even the most bitter enemies must learn to compete peacefully while at Olympia," he says in a singsong voice.

You pass a marble statue of an enormous, muscular man. "Who's that?" you ask the guide.

A look of surprise crosses the tour guide's face. "Do you mean to tell me you don't recognize the greatest athlete of all time?" he asks.

The statue doesn't look like anyone you recognize, but then you remember that all the athletes you know haven't even been born yet! You feel your face growing hot as you shake your head.

"Why this is Milo of Croton, of course," the tour guide says impatiently. "He is the only athlete in the history of the Olympics to have won the wrestling crown six times in a row. To develop his strength he carried a calf on his shoulders for an hour every day until it was a full-grown bull!"

*Turn to page 73.*

# 56

The crowd lifts up you and Athos and carries you to the Temple of Zeus. There, along with the day's other victors, a wreath of wild olive branches is placed on your head. A huge feast of roast bulls has been prepared, and you and Athos sit side by side at the table, both exhausted, both hungrier than you have ever been in your lives, and both champions at Olympia!

Just as you finish eating, the gray-bearded chief Olympic official approaches you and Athos. "Because you were both so impressive in the *skamma* today," he begins. "I would like to invite you to participate in the *pankration* events the day after tomorrow."

"*Pankration?*" you say.

"It means 'game of all powers,'" Athos whispers. "You must know that."

"I do," you say quickly, "but—"

"The *pankration* really is the ultimate athletic test," the official continues, "because it combines wrestling with boxing. No holds are barred, so the competition is often quite violent. But the champion at *pankration* is truly the strongest and most cunning athlete in the world."

*Turn to page 64.*

# 58

You hurry toward the entrance to the cave you've spotted. If it's the cave through which you were brought back in time, you're determined to get back to it before it disappears again. As you walk on the steep incline, you pass many other people, all dressed in togas similar to yours. They look at you strangely as you walk by. They're probably wondering why you're heading away from the procession, you think.

You reach the opening in the hillside. This cave looks different from the one by which you were transported to ancient Greece. The entrance seems much smaller, but perhaps it leads to the same cave. You dash inside.

At once you feel a whirling rush of cold wind, just like the one that carried you back to ancient Greece. But this time you're not afraid. You're certain that at any moment you'll be back with your family. You think you might even be glad to see cousin Felix!

*Turn to page 89.*

Suddenly, the strength races from your body, and a feeling of exhaustion overcomes you. The effects of a day of wrestling catch up with you all at once. Pain rips through your muscles; your legs and arms feel incredibly heavy; it's difficult for you to stand.

Out of the corner of your eye you catch sight of Athos, lying in the sand, staring at you. A strange look crosses his face, and you soon know why. In an instant Athos has figured out what has made you invincible in the wrestling pit. He reaches out and plucks your shining medal from the sand!

There's a change in Athos the moment he clasps the medal. He leaps to his feet, his strength renewed. He doesn't look exhausted anymore, just proud and confident. His body gleams in the late afternoon sun, and on his face is the playful grin of a cat about to catch a mouse.

A ripple of gasps and whispers passes through the crowd. It's clear they've sensed the sudden change in circumstances, although you doubt that anyone has figured out the cause.

Athos doesn't waste any time in claiming his victory. Once . . . twice . . . three times he slams you to the sand, all the while clasping the lion medal. Completely worn out, you're defenseless against Athos and the power of the medal.

The crowd lets loose a deafening cheer as the official raises Athos's arm in victory. But you're too bruised and ashamed even to lift your head.

**The End**

As you try to pass, Demonicus starts to laugh. "Is this the best you could do, Leon?" he says. "You don't seriously expect to win that race tomorrow with a kid driving your chariot!" He gives another horrible laugh.

If there's one thing you really hate, it's being called young. "Go ahead and laugh," you shout. "We'll see who's laughing when I finish first tomorrow!"

Demonicus fixes his hard, icy stare on you. "You'll be lucky, kid, if you finish at all."

You lead the chariot inside, the sound of Demonicus's laughter fading into the distance. "We'd better keep watch over the horses and the chariot tonight," Leon says. "Demonicus was expecting me to drop out of the race, and I wouldn't be surprised if he tries again to keep us from competing."

Together you decide that Leon will stand guard for the first half of the night, and you'll keep watch for the second. After a quick dinner, you sleep for several hours in the athletes' quarters. When you wake up you head back to the stable to relieve Leon. He tells you that all is well.

*Go on to the next page.*

For the next hour you don't hear a sound other than the horses breathing. It's after four o'clock in the morning, and you're still pretty tired. You'd really like to get some more sleep—it's important to be rested for the race. Surely if Demonicus and his men were going to try anything, they'd have come by now. Even if they were to come while you were sleeping, you're pretty sure you'd hear them and wake up. But what if you didn't? Maybe it's better to force yourself to stay awake.

*If you decide to get a little more sleep,*
*turn to page 97.*

*If you try your hardest to stay awake,*
*turn to page 85.*

"Don't worry about him," Leon says to you after Demonicus's chariot has passed. "He's only trying to scare us. Keep your mind on the race, and you'll do fine."

Demonicus *has* scared you, but he's also strengthened your resolve. You're going to do your best to win back Leon's daughter, even if it's the last thing you do!

You arrive at the Hippodrome and join in the procession across the course to the starting gate. Thousands of people are gathered on the embankment alongside the Hippodrome, cheering wildly for their favorite chariot owners and racers.

You feel a rush of excitement as you drive your chariot into the stall you've been assigned in the V-shaped starting gate. Leon wishes you luck and gets down from the chariot. Then, with your whip poised, you focus all of your attention on the bronze eagle on an altar at the center of the starting gate. When the eagle flies into the air, the race will begin.

It takes a few more minutes for all of the chariots to get into the starting gate. Then everything happens very quickly: a trumpet blasts, the bronze eagle jerks upward, and the rope at the front of your stall falls to the ground. The race is on!

*Turn to page 22.*

# 64

You're not sure what to do. It's beyond your wildest dreams to be declared the best athlete in the world. But you've never even heard of *pankration* before, and it sounds terribly dangerous.

"If you're thinking of competing, you should probably consult the Olympic oracle to help make up your mind," the official continues, sensing your uncertainty. "But if you're not interested in *pankration,* you can always watch the rest of the events from the special area reserved for champions."

*If you decide to consult the Olympic oracle about the* pankration, *turn to page 31.*

*If you decide to watch the other events, turn to page 70.*

You follow the shaggy-bearded man up the hill. After a few minutes he stops beside a brook and drinks a couple of handfuls of water. Then he walks on at a slow pace. You wish he would hurry. There isn't much time before the start of the race, and Leon must already be wondering what's happened to you.

A short while later, the man stops and looks around. He seems to be cautious about something. Could he be making sure no one is following him? You hide behind a tree until he starts to walk again. You're now on the far side of the hill, away from the main campsite.

Just then a trumpet fanfare rings out, summoning the chariots to the Hippodrome. But you can't leave now; you're certain that in just a few minutes you'll find Leon's daughter. Meanwhile the man stops and looks off into the distance, using his hand to shade his eyes. Is he searching for a signal of some sort?

Finally he walks down the hill at a quick pace, obviously with some destination in mind. Looking ahead, you see a tent with a man sitting next to it. He must be keeping watch over Marissa!

*Turn to page 106.*

"Follow me!" you say and, dodging around the racing chariots, you lead him safely out of the Hippodrome.

You watch happily as Leon is reunited with his daughter.

"I will see to it that Demonicus is brought to justice," Leon promises. "Marissa and I will go straight to the Temple of Zeus to talk to the chief Olympic priest. The remains of my chariot and our testimony should be enough to convince the priest of Demonicus's guilt."

You say good-bye to your friends, and as they start off toward the Temple of Zeus, you hear Felix calling you. You'd forgotten all about him! He asks you where you're going.

"To look for the cave," you say. "It's definitely time to try to get back home. Want to come?"

"Sure," Felix replies. "Let's go."

## The End

If a chariot race isn't the place for taking chances, what is? you think, as you summon all your courage, give a wild shout, and crack your whip. The horses surge forward, drawing you into the oncoming pack. The other chariots are frighteningly close, but miraculously, you make it through unharmed.

Now your chariot is flying down the length of the field. The area directly ahead of you is completely free. You glance behind you, expecting to see Demonicus's chariot in hot pursuit, but you don't see it anywhere.

You slow down to drive around the pole, then draw to the right of the field. Before you entered the turn, the nearest chariot was half a field behind you, so you have time to be cautious now.

As you again pass the pack of chariots, you don't see Nikos at all. What's happened to him? you wonder.

You don't have to go much farther to find out. Fifty yards down the field you see Nikos standing in the dirt next to his chariot. He's waving his arms wildly at another driver, whose chariot has collided with his. As you draw past, you see that one of the wheels of Demonicus's chariot has fallen off in the accident. It serves him right, you think, urging your horses on at full speed.

*Turn to page 116.*

# 68

You arrive at a fountain just outside the Olympic grounds, where the athletes have formed into a long line. At the front of the group are stern-faced men in purple robes, who wear crowns of wild olive branches. They seem to be in charge, so you figure that these must be officials of some sort.

One of the men waves and a fanfare of trumpets blares out. As you step back to join the large crowd that has gathered by the side of the road, the procession begins to move. Dozens of trumpeters file past, playing a stirring march. Next come the athletes, divided into groups according to the sport in which they will participate. First come the wrestlers and boxers; then come the runners, looking tall and graceful. A group of strong-armed discus throwers marches by next, followed by teams of horses pulling chariots.

As the next group approaches, a bald man standing near you says, "Why haven't you joined the procession to the Temple of Zeus? Here come the youths now. Hurry! Take your place!"

There must be some mistake, you think. Is this man confusing you with one of the athletes? You turn and see that a group of boys and girls really is approaching. Imagine being able to compete in the Olympics! All your friends back home would turn green with envy. You think that you might be able to slip into the procession without being noticed. But what will happen to you if somebody notices that you don't belong? With just a moment's hesitation you step into the road and join the procession.

*Turn to page 76*.

For the next two days, you and Athos decide to see as many of the athletic competitions at Olympia as you can. To see the running events you go to the stadium at the foot of the Hill of Cronus.

"Wow," you gasp when you see the size of the field. "This place is huge!"

An old man standing next to you smiles and says, "Legend has it that Hercules himself determined the length of the stadium by seeing how far he could run on one lungful of air."

Hercules must have been incredibly strong, you realize. The stadium at Olympia is more than twice the length of a football field!

The last of the running events at Olympia is a race called the *hoplite,* which requires the participants to run two lengths of the stadium in battle armor. The runners wear heavy, feathered helmets, metal breastplates and leg guards, and carry round wooden shields. Some of the contestants collide with one another during the race, and the crowd howls with laughter at the sight of the burdened runners lumbering down the field.

*Go on to the next page.*

Still laughing, you and Athos head for the boxing competition. This event is held at the Palestra, and is very different from twentieth-century boxing. There are no rounds or rest periods, and the boxers don't wear gloves; instead they wrap each of their hands with oiled leather thongs. The matches go on until one of the opponents gives up or is knocked out. A couple of matches go on so long that the referee orders a "climax." When this happens the boxers take turns hitting each other until one of them gives up the fight. By this point the contestants are bruised and bleeding, and a couple even have broken bones!

*Turn to page 80.*

"The old wax-pin trick," says the bearded man, giving a low chuckle. "Does it really work?"

"Every time," the man with the scar replies. "After a few minutes of racing the pins melt, and off fly the wheels!"

"It's too bad Demonicus wants to stick around for the race," says the first man. "He might as well leave Olympia with Marissa tonight. There's no way now that Leon and his driver are going to win!"

You're horrified by what you hear. But as the two men put the chariot away, something one of them said registers within your mind. The bearded man thought that Demonicus should leave Olympia right away with Marissa: that means Leon's daughter is somewhere on the Olympic grounds!

If you follow the two men, maybe they'll lead you to Marissa. But will you be able to rescue her all by yourself? you wonder. From what you know of Demonicus, you shudder to think what he would do if he caught you. And what if the men don't lead you to Marissa? You might miss the chariot race and give up any chance of winning her back! Maybe it would be better to put the chariot back to the way it was and surprise Demonicus by finishing the race—maybe in first place.

*If you decide to follow the men, turn to page 19.*

*If you think it's better to stay at the stable, turn to page 108.*

You pass many buildings and statues and hear the tour guide's fascinating stories about ancient Olympians. He tells you about Polydamus of Thessaly, who was so strong that with one hand he could stop a chariot driving past at full speed. Then he tells the story of Oebotus of Achaia, who put a curse on his city-state because he was unhappy with the celebration it gave him when he returned from Olympia. For more than three centuries, no Achaian won a single event in the Olympics. Finally, the city built a statue in Oebotus's honor, and once more citizens of Achaia began to win at Olympia.

*Turn to page 75.*

The tour guide leads you to the enormous white marble Temple of Zeus at the center of the Olympian plain. The temple has been built to honor the most powerful and awesome of the Greek gods. Just inside the temple you see an immense ivory and gold statue of Zeus seated on a huge cedar throne adorned with gold and jewels. Your guide tells you that the statue has just been completed in time for this Olympic festival, and already it has been proclaimed one of the Seven Wonders of the World.

As your tour group begins to move on, you linger before the statue, the first thing you recognize from your lessons about Greece in school. Suddenly you notice two men in deep purple togas talking in a dark corner of the temple. One of the men reaches behind a column and pulls out something that looks like a sword. Your guide told you that all weapons are forbidden at Olympia. Are these men trying to disrupt the games? Every citizen of ancient Greece is expected to guard the law. And for the moment you're a citizen of ancient Greece.

"Stop those men!" you shout, pointing toward the temple.

Your tour group whirls around, but no one makes a move.

"They've got swords!" you cry. "Stop them!"

*Turn to page 48.*

The procession winds its way through Olympia. On either side of the road, cheering crowds chant the names of their city-states and their favorite athletes. As you walk by them you feel proud to be taking part in such an important event.

The procession stops as you reach the tallest and most impressive building on the Olympian field. It's the columned building you thought looked like the Parthenon. You look inside the building and see a gigantic statue of a seated god. This must be the Temple of Zeus.

One of the purple-robed men who had led the procession stands before the temple. He directs the athletes to take an oath pledging to compete honestly and to the best of their ability. You raise your right hand and take the oath.

The group of athletes begins to break up, but you're not sure what to do next. You see a boy about your age, and you decide to talk to him. After you introduce yourself the boy tells you he is Athos, from the city-state of Heraea, in northern Greece. "Where do you come from?" he asks.

"Uh . . . Americos," you say after a moment's hesitation.

"Americos?" says Athos. "I've never heard of that city-state. Is it near Athens?"

"No," you answer. "It's in the west . . . over by Mexicos and Canadas."

*Go on to the next page.*

Athos shrugs and explains that he is on his way to register for the competition. "I've come to Olympia to wrestle," he says. "What are you here for?"

A dozen thoughts go through your head. What sport should you say? You're strong for your age; you might do very well at wrestling. But then again, you've always loved horses, and you'll surely never have another chance to enter a chariot race.

*If you say, "Wrestling," turn to page 88.*

*If you say, "Chariot racing," turn to page 44.*

The first stars have appeared in the sky when you and Leon arrive at the long rows of stables. You stop at Leon's stable to pick up a lantern, then walk on. The area seems deserted, and the only sounds you hear are your own footsteps and the occasional whinny of a horse.

"This is it," Leon whispers as you reach Demonicus's stable. "Now wait out here while I go inside. I should be gone for only a few minutes. If you hear or see anyone coming, rap softly on the door. I'll try to get away through another exit, and we'll meet back at my stable. Otherwise, I'll see you here."

The stable door creaks as Leon opens it. Without another word he slips silently into the darkness inside.

A minute passes as you wait nervously, straining your ears for sounds of anyone approaching. A breeze rustles the leaves on the trees, making it difficult for you to concentrate. But when the wind dies, you hear the unmistakable sound of footsteps. And it sounds as if more than one person is coming directly toward you!

Instantly you tap on the door, signaling Leon to escape. By now the footsteps have gotten closer, and at the far end of the stable you see the glow of a torch. You don't want to be seen here, but you're not sure if there's enough time to run away. Maybe you should sneak inside the stable instead and try to find the exit Leon used.

*If you run, turn to page 23.*

*If you go into the stable, turn to page 21.*

You've had fun in ancient Greece, but you think you should be getting back to the twentieth century. You walk up the steep incline of the Hill of Cronus. As you draw nearer to the cave, the light from the opening seems to be dimmer. With a start you realize the entrance is closing! You race toward the light, trying to avoid the bushes and rocks on the hillside. By the time you reach it, the cave opening is just wide enough for you to slip through.

The eerie light inside the cave has a hypnotic effect on you. Your body feels weightless, and you can barely feel your feet touching the ground. You're in a state somewhere between waking and dreaming as a whirlwind blast of air surrounds you. It's almost as if you're watching everything from a distance, yet you know you're not.

Gradually sensation returns to your body. You see that it's daytime, and you're standing on a hill. Below you, Olympia lies in ruins.

Your cousin Felix comes running up to you. "I've been looking all over for you. It's time to get back on the bus," he yells. "Hey, what's that on your head?" he says.

*Turn to page 29.*

On the fifth and last day of the festival, you and Athos are proud to join the other champions parading through the grounds of Olympia. The crowds that line the path shower you with flowers and olive leaves. Finally the procession reaches the Temple of Zeus. Inside the temple you watch the high priests of Olympia, the *Hellanodicae,* place a huge olive-branch crown on the statue of Zeus to signify his reign over the other gods.

The Olympic festival is now over. You overhear a man explaining to his daughter that the truce among the Greek city-states will continue for another month, until everyone has returned home safely. "In the city-states of the Olympic champions, great celebrations will take place," the man explains. "The citizens will knock down a portion of the walls surrounding the city, and the athlete will enter through this opening. This is done to show that a city-state in which an Olympic champion lives has no need of walls to protect it against its enemies."

You say good-bye to Athos and wish him a safe journey home. You look at the statue of Zeus and wish that your trip to the Olympics would last forever.

Just then your arms and legs begin to tingle and grow stiff. You try to move your head, but your neck seems to be frozen in place. Every part of your body feels as cold and heavy as stone.

Little did you realize the terrible power of the king of the Greek gods. Zeus has granted your wish: you have turned into a marble statue, and you'll stay at Olympia until the end of time.

**The End**

You spend the entire next day learning how to command the horses and drive the chariot. The race will require you to drive up and down the length of the Hippodrome twenty-four times. You know it will be grueling, but Leon is an excellent teacher, and by sunset you feel confident about your racing skills.

On the morning of the race you wake up early and hitch the horses to the chariot. When you hear a signal from the trumpets at the Hippodrome, you and Leon start to drive the chariot to the racecourse.

On the way, Leon hands you a small leather pouch. "Take this," he says. "It contains a lock of my daughter's hair. Four years ago, the driver who raced my chariot against Demonicus's carried the pouch with him and won. Perhaps this will also bring you good luck."

You thank Leon and tie the cord that closes the pouch around one of the reins. Just then another chariot, drawn by four jet-black stallions, catches up to yours. The driver is strong and muscular. At his side is a sinister-looking man with a bald head and bushy gray eyebrows. As the chariot draws near, his cold, piercing dark eyes glare at you. You've never seen anyone look so cunning. You know at once that this is Demonicus.

*Go on to the next page.*

"Going for a little drive, Leon?" Demonicus says. He gives a vicious laugh. "If you're heading for the Hippodrome, I hope your driver has an appetite for dust."

As if to drive home his point, Demonicus takes the whip from his driver and urges his horses forward. They pass your chariot, raising a blinding cloud of dust and sand. You can barely see Demonicus now, but the horrible sound of his laughter is perfectly clear.

*Turn to page 62.*

You try every trick you know in order to keep from falling asleep: whistling your favorite songs, running in place, counting to a thousand. Finally the sky begins to lighten; in only another couple of hours the chariot race will begin. In the meantime, you decide to remember all fifty states. But just as you're trying to remember which state is south of South Dakota, you hear footsteps and some whispering outside the stable.

You leap to your feet and crouch down behind a pile of hay. The door to the stable creaks open, and the footsteps draw closer. Over the top of the hay, you see two men approaching. One has long black hair and a shaggy beard; the other has short curly hair and a jagged scar on his left cheek. You recognize them at once: two of Demonicus's henchmen!

Without a word, the men walk toward the compartment where the chariot is stored and pull it into the open. Then the scarred man takes something out from under his toga. It looks like a crude wrench. With it, he removes the pins that hold the chariot's wheels in place. He tosses them into a dark corner of the stable, then he replaces the pins with another set the other man has handed to him. What's going on? you wonder.

*Turn to page 72.*

You head down a long corridor, and soon you're before Demonicus's door. But how are you going to rescue Marissa? you wonder.

The scar-faced man is much bigger than you, so you wouldn't be much of a match for him in a fight. And you can't let him see you because he might recognize you from the Hippodrome. There must be some way to outwit him.

Just then you have an idea. If you can lure the man out of the room, maybe you could distract him and rush inside to rescue Marissa. It's a desperate plan, but it just might work.

You take a clay urn from a pedestal in the hallway. Then you knock on Demonicus's door and hide behind a pillar. A moment later you hear footsteps on the other side of the door, then the sound of the door opening. The man mutters something under his breath when he discovers that no one is there. Just then you take the urn and hurl it to the floor. It shatters with a terrible crash.

*Turn to page 90.*

Your vision blurs, and the last thing you see is Sarapion raising his hand in defeat. It's too late for you—you haven't got the strength to fight back. Sarapion's stranglehold will be fatal. The oracle was right: You've found doom as well as victory in the *pankration,* and your corpse will be crowned with a wreath of olive branches.

**The End**

"So you're a wrestler, too," says Athos. "Let's go to register together."

You go to a low square building behind the Temple of Zeus. This is the Palestra, the wrestling school. At the center of the building is a large courtyard containing a sand pit, which Athos calls the *skamma*.

You give your name to the official seated behind a table, a heavy-set scowling woman with a double chin. She looks as though she might be a wrestler herself. She searches through a large scroll of names, but can't find yours anywhere.

"I'm a late entry," you explain. "I just arrived at Olympia."

"Another one," says the woman, still scowling. "You don't happen to know someone named Felicitus, do you?" You shake your head. "He was a late entry, too," she says. Then she explains that the wrestling events will be held at the Palestra the next morning.

As you walk away Athos asks you to come inside the Palestra to practice your wrestling. Maybe you'll be able to pick up some pointers from him. You'll need to learn more about wrestling if you're going to compete tomorrow.

*Turn to page 28.*

A moment later you hear a familiar voice calling your name. Your head feels very heavy, as if you've been asleep for a long time. You sit up and see bright morning sunlight streaming through the window of your bedroom. That's funny . . . you're still wearing your toga. You must have fallen asleep in it the night before.

You shake your head to clear your thoughts. What strange dreams you've had. You remember your family visiting a place that looked just like Olympia, only all of the buildings were in ruins . . . and you had traveled there in a birdlike vehicle that flew through the air over the sea. You remember that everyone was wearing the oddest-looking togas you'd ever seen. And there was some nonsense about a cave that could transport you through time . . .

You hear your name being called once again. It's your mother, telling you that breakfast is ready. "Hurry!" she says. "You must set out for Olympia soon."

Olympia . . . of course! You were so concerned about your dreams that you'd nearly forgotten. Today is the day you must join the other young athletes from your city-state and begin the long march to Olympia. The Olympic festival begins in three days, and you've been chosen to compete there. Without a further thought about your dreams, you jump out of bed and get ready for breakfast.

**The End**

As you'd hoped, the man starts to investigate. When he passes the pillar, you rush out, shove him to the ground, and race into the room, bolting the door behind you! A beautiful woman with long brown hair is sitting by the window, a frightened look on her face. It's Marissa!

"I come from your father," you say quickly, and Marissa's face lights up. There's no time to explain any further; the man with the scar is already pounding on the door. "Quick! Out the window!" you say. A moment later the two of you are outside and rushing toward Leon's stable.

Just then a fanfare of trumpets rings out. It's the signal for the chariots to gather at the Hippodrome for the start of the race. Suddenly a horrible thought occurs to you: What if Leon has decided to drive his own chariot in the race? "We'd better hurry," you say. "There's not a second to lose!"

*Turn to page 98.*

You remove the medal from around your neck and place it on the bench alongside your oil jar and *strigil.*

An official in a purple robe calls you and Athos to the center of the *skamma.* The two of you stand on either side of him, and he clasps one hand on your shoulder and the other on Athos's. "These two youths are the finest wrestlers in the world," he announces. "Now let us see which one is best."

The official leaves the *skamma* and gives the signal for you to begin wrestling. You and Athos start to circle each other, arms extended, looking for just the right moment to make your first move. But as you circle, your body starts to feel strange: your arms grow heavy, your legs feel rubbery, and you're suddenly very tired. It's as if the day's wrestling has caught up with you all at once. As you feared, taking off the medal has made you terribly weak.

Suddenly Athos lunges forward and grabs you by the leg. You've got to concentrate on your wrestling; otherwise you're sure to lose. At this point in the competition, Athos is as weak and tired as you. You pivot to avoid falling, and manage to escape his hold.

*Turn to page 13.*

The fire rises higher. For a second you worry that your sacrifice is not acceptable to the oracle. But then the fire dies down, and the last lick of flame disappears.

A bluish light begins to glow within the cavern, and you see that it illuminates a set of wide stone stairs leading underground. You enter the cavern and go down the stairs, which are slippery with moss. The wind still blows into the cavern, but now it makes a sound like voices chanting in some strange language.

You follow the stairs down to a huge empty chamber. Just then the bluish glow, which seems to come from the stone walls themselves, begins to fade, and a shaft of golden light from above illuminates a recess at the far end of the chamber. Standing in the recess is a tall woman wearing a beautiful blue gown: the priestess of the oracle!

"What is it you wish?" the priestess asks, and the wind around you seems to echo her question.

"I want to know whether I will be victorious in the *pankration*," you manage to say.

The voices in the wind begin to laugh, and the golden light above the priestess turns to red. The priestess's body stiffens, and she starts to rock back and forth in a trance, her fingers outstretched like claws, her head tilted back. Is this what is supposed to happen, you wonder frantically, or have you offended the oracle in some way?

*Turn to page 6.*

It would be dishonest to take back the medal, so you leave it lying where you found it. As you walk away from the cavern of the oracle, the wall of flames rises up behind you, blocking the entrance again.

During your journey back to Olympia, you think about the oracle's prophecy. The priestess said that you would win the competition, but that the victory would be surrounded by doom. What can that mean? you wonder. How can winning the most challenging athletic competition in the ancient world possibly bring doom?

You're still wondering about the oracle's mysterious prediction as you approach Olympia. Just then you see an odd light on the Hill of Cronus. It's coming from an opening in the hillside—a cave!

As you walk closer to the hill, you become more certain that the light is coming from the same cave through which you were transported back in time. Maybe now is your chance to get back to the twentieth century. But what about competing in the *pankration*? Should you be content with your wrestling victory, or should you try to win more Olympic glory—even if it means risking the doom the oracle foretold?

*If you try to enter the cave, turn to page 79.*

*If you decide to compete in the* pankration, *turn to page 47.*

"That's terrible," you say to Leon. "But how can *I* help you?"

"I am in an awful predicament," he answers sadly. "If I compete fairly and race my own chariot against Nikos, I will surely lose. There's no way an old man like me could win against the best charioteer in the world. And all the best drivers have already agreed to race for other chariot owners. Although it shames me to say it, I'm afraid the only way to get my daughter back is to compete unfairly. Somehow I must win that race. The only way is to make sure Nikos loses. I think I can arrange that, if I can get into the stables unnoticed and sabotage Demonicus's chariot. For the sake of my daughter, will you help me?"

You're not sure what to say. On the one hand you understand why Leon is so desperate, but he wants to cheat and that's wrong. On the other hand, it wasn't fair of Demonicus to seize Leon's daughter and then spoil Leon's chances of winning her back.

Just then another thought comes to you. Leon might be too old to race his chariot, but *you* certainly aren't! Why couldn't you enter the race? But wait a minute! You've never even ridden in a chariot before. What chance do you have of driving successfully against Nikos of Sparta? And if you lose, Leon will never see Marissa again. Maybe you *should* help to sabotage the chariot.

---

*If you want to help Leon sabotage Demonicus's chariot, turn to page 109.*

*If you volunteer to ride for Leon, turn to page 8.*

You're certain that a few hours more rest will make a big difference in your racing, so you walk over to a low haystack and lie down. Soon all worries about Demonicus disappear as you fall into a deep sleep.

You have a strange dream about your cousin Felix: you and he are in a chariot race, but for some reason, instead of riding in the chariots, you're pulling them! And just when you reach the finish line and win the race, a rooster begins to crow. And the harder you tell it to stop, the louder it crows.

Suddenly you're startled from your sleep. That rooster wasn't just in your dream, it's real! Sunlight is streaming through the windows at the end of the stable, and the rooster is crowing louder than ever. You didn't mean to fall asleep for so long; it's almost time for the race!

You look quickly around the stable to see if anything has been touched while you were asleep. The horses look fine, the chariot is still in its compartment, and the bridles and reins are hanging on the wall where you left them. What's more, you feel full of energy. Taking that nap wasn't such a bad idea after all.

*Turn to page 41.*

A quick look inside the stables when you and Marissa arrive confirms your worst fear: both Leon and the horses are gone. You guess that when Leon came back to the stable and didn't find you, he assumed you'd deserted him—or even that you were kidnapped. He didn't want to waste his one chance at winning back his daughter, so he decided to drive the chariot himself. But Leon doesn't know that Demonicus's henchmen have tampered with the chariot's wheels. Unless you can get to him something awful will happen!

Marissa deserves to know of the danger to her father, so you quickly explain. But just as you finish you hear a familiar voice calling your name. It can't be . . . Sure enough, it is. Your cousin Felix is running straight toward you. How did he get here?

You don't even have to ask. "I saw you go into that cave, so I decided to follow," Felix explains, out of breath. "Then I couldn't find you, and someone asked me to enter one of the running contests. And look"—he points to the olive-branch crown on his head—"I won!"

"If your friend here is so fast," Marissa says excitedly, "maybe the two of you can run to the Hippodrome before the race starts."

You're not so sure about Marissa's idea. Speed is crucial, but can you trust him to help save Leon, or will he just get in the way as usual? Maybe you should run to the Hippodrome yourself instead.

*If you take Felix along, turn to page 25.*

*If you try to save Leon yourself,
turn to page 46.*

Quickly you hitch the horses to the chariot and drive with Leon to the gates of the Hippodrome. You take your place in the procession and make your way to your assigned stall in the starting gate. Leon steps down from the chariot and wishes you luck.

Demonicus's chariot, pulled by four jet-black stallions, enters the stall next to yours. Demonicus has a wicked gleam in his eyes as he talks to his driver, Nikos of Sparta. No doubt he's telling Nikos what his henchmen have done to your chariot. But you've got a surprise for him!

All of the chariots are now in place. With the reins in one hand and your whip in the other, you focus on the bronze eagle at the front of the starting gate. A trumpet blast rings out, and the eagle soars into the air. The race has begun.

*Turn to page 22.*

It's hard to take your mind off the plans to sabotage Demonicus's chariot, but you watch the trumpeting competition anyway. The first contest determines who can hold a note for the longest time. With a wave of his hand an official directs all of the trumpeters to blow into their horns. The shrill sound of twenty trumpets blowing at once makes you want to cover your ears. One by one the trumpeters run out of breath. Finally only one trumpeter, a barrel-chested, red-faced man named Herodorus, continues to hold the note. When at last he can blow no more, the crowd bursts into applause.

Throughout the afternoon, Herodorus places first in every part of the contest. He blows the highest and lowest notes, and plays the most beautiful melody. And he clinches his victory at the end of the competition by playing two trumpets at once!

By the time Herodorus is declared the official Olympic trumpeter, the sun has sunk low and the sky is beginning to darken. "Come," says Leon. "It's time to go to the stables."

*Turn to page 78.*

An instant later, all is still. You get to your feet, realizing that you're again wearing your comfortable pair of jeans and favorite T-shirt. You look around you and see that you're standing on the Hill of Cronus, overlooking the Olympic ruins. Everything is just as it was before you entered the cave.

At the bottom of the hill, someone is calling you. It's your cousin Felix, and he's telling you it's time to get back on the tour bus. "I'll be right there," you shout down to him.

Have you really traveled through time, or was your adventure just an incredible daydream? you wonder as you start to walk down the hill. Then something on the ground glistens in the light. It's your medal! You really were in ancient Greece!

You remember Apollo's punishment, and you know that you should probably leave the medal exactly where you found it. But then you think about the incredible strength the medal brought you. It might just come in handy some day. Besides, no one believes in Apollo anymore; he probably doesn't have any power in your own time. You'll take your chances. Without another thought you scoop up the medal, put it into your pocket, and hurry down the hill to meet your family.

**The End**

Suddenly you realize that Demonicus must have come into the stable while you were sleeping last night, and tampered with the pins that held your wheels in place. The last thing you see is Demonicus's chariot speeding toward you. Luckily you lose consciousness just before his horses trample you to death.

**The End**

# 104

The crowd lets loose an enormous cheer as Sarapion springs on top of you. Then you feel his hands close around your throat. He's got you in a stranglehold!

You try to pull Sarapion's hands off your neck, but his grip tightens. Your lungs are straining, and your head begins to feel very light.

You reach down desperately and grab hold of Sarapion's ankle. With your last bit of strength, you twist as hard as you can. Sarapion lets loose a cry of pain.

*Turn to page 87*.

When the shaggy-bearded man arrives at the tent, you crouch low in the tall grass, trying to remain hidden as you approach. You rack your brains to think of a way to outwit the two men and seize Leon's daughter. But when one of the men draws open the tent, you see that no one else is inside. You've followed the wrong man. And the second blast of trumpets you hear just then tells you that the chariot race has begun! You've lost your chance to rescue Marissa before Demonicus takes her away from Olympia for good!

## The End

At the end of the hearing you stand before the chief priest. "Cheating will never be allowed at Olympia, and those who cheat must always be punished," he says in a solemn voice. "At the foot of the Hill of Cronus, you will see the statues of athletes who have cheated in the past. These are called *zanes*. As your punishment, you must carve a statue of yourself that will stand at Olympia until the end of time. On the base you will inscribe the following: 'Not by cheating, but with speed of foot and strength of body must prizes be won at Olympia.'"

You spend the entire night carving your *zane*. As you work, people stop to laugh at you. You've never felt more embarrassed in your life. You only hope you can locate the cave through which you were brought back in time and somehow find your way back home. You don't want to spend another minute in ancient Greece!

**The End**

You stay hidden behind the haystack until the two men have left the stable. Then you search through the straw on the ground until you find the iron pins the scarred man tossed aside. You take the chariot out once again and replace the wax pins. You're hammering the last iron pin in place when Leon enters the stable.

"What are you doing?" he asks. "Is something wrong with the chariot?"

You explain what Demonicus's henchmen tried to do. Leon shakes his head sadly. "Demonicus will stop at nothing to win the race," he says. "Who knows what he'll try next when he discovers this trick hasn't worked? One way or another he'll get us. Maybe we should drop out now—before something terrible happens."

But you're not about to be intimidated. You won't let Demonicus get away with kidnapping Marissa or with trying to sabotage Leon's chariot. "No," you declare. "We've come this far together; we can't give up now."

Just then you hear a fanfare of trumpets ring out. It's the signal for all of the contestants to gather at the gates of the Hippodrome. The chariot race is about to begin!

*Turn to page 99.*

"All right, I'll help you with the chariot," you say.

"Good," says Leon. "I was hoping I could count on you. We'll wait until nightfall before we go out to the stables. We're less likely to be noticed then. In the meantime, let's watch the trumpeting contest."

You follow Leon back to the Temple of Zeus. A crowd has gathered around a low platform there, and on the platform, about twenty men and women hold long brass horns.

"Trumpeting is very important here at Olympia," Leon tells you. "The winner of today's competition will use his trumpet to start all of the races during the festival. Winning the contest is a very big honor."

*Turn to page 101.*

# 110

You crack your whip once again and tug on the reins to accelerate. The chariot bounces as the horses fly forward, but you hold on tightly. The cloud of dust over the field is thick now, making it hard to breathe and even harder to see.

You narrowly beat Nikos to the pole at the end of the course where the race began. Your chariot skids dangerously to the outside as you maneuver a turn, and you're lucky not to be thrown off balance. But the bad turn has slowed you down. As you head once again into the straightaway, Nikos is drawing closer than ever. You hear him screaming furiously at his horses, and their pounding hooves aren't far behind you.

The pack of chariots is approaching again at full speed. Through the dust you think you see a narrow passage. If you can make it through, you'll be able to maintain your lead, but it could turn out to be a disastrous choice. Veering left and going around the pack would be safer. You may lose some ground, but at least you'll have the rest of the race to get it back. You have only a split second to decide.

*If you continue straight through the pack,
turn to page 67.*

*If you avoid the oncoming chariots,
turn to page 114.*

# 112

The sun is at its highest point when you arrive at the Palestra. Already a huge crowd—much larger than the one at the wrestling events—is assembled around the sand pit in the central courtyard.

You take your place on the bench alongside the *pankratiasts,* and try to size up the competition. Some of the other athletes are much bigger than you, but you doubt that they're as crafty or agile. And you're sure that no one is more determined to win than you.

As in wrestling, the *pankratiasts* are divided into two groups. The group that you're not in draws the names of its opponents from a silver bowl. There are an odd number of competitors, and no one selects your name. You receive a "dustless victory," and don't have to compete until the second round. Already you feel that luck is going your way, since your first opponent will be worn out from competing.

After sitting through the first round of the *pankration,* you finally get your turn to compete. Your opponent is a tough-looking boy from Thasos named Sarapion. You put oil and sand on your body, then take your place opposite him in the *skamma.*

---

*Go on to the next page.*

When the official gives the sign to start, Sarapion moves closer to you. He lashes a swift kick at your stomach, but you're able to back off in time and grab his foot. Caught off balance, Sarapion tumbles to the sand.

Instantly you fall to your knees and attempt to pin down his shoulders. But Sarapion grabs a handful of sand and throws it right into your eyes! You're blinded and helpless, and Sarapion has escaped your grip!

*Turn to page 104.*

Better safe than sorry, you think as you steer your chariot to the left around the oncoming pack. But just as you've passed the group of chariots, you're stunned to see a lone chariot coming straight toward you!

There's no time to think. To avoid a collision, you tug on the left set of reins with all your might. You just miss smashing into the other chariot, but your horses are going too fast to manage the turn. In an instant, your chariot tips over, spilling you out onto the course. The horses rear up in fear, then continue running, unaware that you're no longer in command.

Luckily you're uninjured. You get to your feet and run off the course just in time to avoid an oncoming chariot. But you've lost the race. All you can do is wait and hope that Demonicus will have mercy on Leon and safely return his daughter.

**The End**

The remaining chariots are no competition for yours. In what seems only a matter of minutes, you drive the twenty-fourth lap of the Hippodrome and cross the finish line in first place!

An enormous cheer goes up from the crowd, and you feel overcome by a mixture of joy, pride, and relief. Leon rushes up as you dismount from the chariot. You've never seen anyone look happier.

"You did it!" he shouts. He throws his arms around you and raises one of your arms in victory. Again the crowd cheers. It's the most exciting moment of your life.

But then Leon's face grows serious. "There's some unsettled business I must take care of now," he says solemnly, and strides away.

A few minutes later Leon returns, a beautiful brown-haired girl at his side. Once again, he looks as if he's about to burst with happiness.

"This is my daughter, Marissa," Leon says, tears of joy in his eyes. "Come, it's time for the victory feast. All three of us have much to celebrate!"

**The End**

## ABOUT THE AUTHOR

BEN M. BAGLIO was born in New York and grew up in a suburb of Philadelphia. He attended the University of Pennsylvania, where he studied English literature. An editor of children's books, Mr. Baglio has worked both in New York City, where he lives, and in England. *The First Olympics* is his first book.

## ABOUT THE ILLUSTRATOR

LESLIE MORRILL is a designer and illustrator whose work has won him numerous awards. He has illustrated over thirty books for children, including the Bantam Classic edition of *The Wind in the Willows*. Mr. Morrill has illustrated many books in the Skylark Choose Your Own Adventure series, and *Lost on the Amazon, Mountain Survival, Invaders of the Planet Earth,* and *The Brilliant Dr. Wogan,* in the Choose Your Own Adventure series. Mr. Morrill also illustrated both Super Adventure books *Journey to the Year 3000* and *Danger Zones.*